ENCHANTED

The illustrations in this book are
paintings by Pattie Brooks Anderson
completed from 2008 to 2011.
The story, written in 2012,
was inspired by them.

"It's as if I could see what it meant to be a part of something whole and so much bigger than
"just me". As long as I do my part, I'm in a great big wonderful complex dance--
I may not be able to see the other dancers, nor can I tell you what the story is, but my part is
vital--as is yours."   *Shelia Conner 2012*

I would like to extend my appreciation to my writing
group, CC Writers, who were instrumental in making
this book a reality. My natural inclination is to think
in pictures and not words, so your suggestions and
encoragement each time we meet has
been inspirational.

By: Pattie Brooks Anderson,
Copyright: 2012, Florence, Oregon,
pattieba1@mac.com

This story is written for my
wonderful grandchildren,
Kyle, Shelby, Siena, Emilia and Gannon,
who inspire me every day---

May you always find enchantment in life.

With Lots of Love, Grandma Pattie

Pattie Brooks Anderson

ENCHANT
transitive verb
1: to influence by, or as if by, charms and incantation
2: to attract and move deeply: rouse to ecstatic admiration

It began on an ordinary day, when a strange wind
blew through the forest.

The snow geese felt this mysterious wind. It alarmed them and they took off, flapping their way into the sky.

Even the insects sensed it. They climbed up from the forest floor to see what was happening. The sky had turned a vibrant pink and the trees were swaying in the wind, as if they were dancing.

Those in the cities and towns of the faraway land felt the change in the atmosphere. The people heard the wind. It sounded like a deep howling. They shivered and felt a chill from this strange disturbance. They wondered what it possibly could be, and they knew that something deeply elemental had changed.

Back in the forest, thunder cracked and the ground shook violently. Planets swirled in the sky and moved dangerously close to the land.

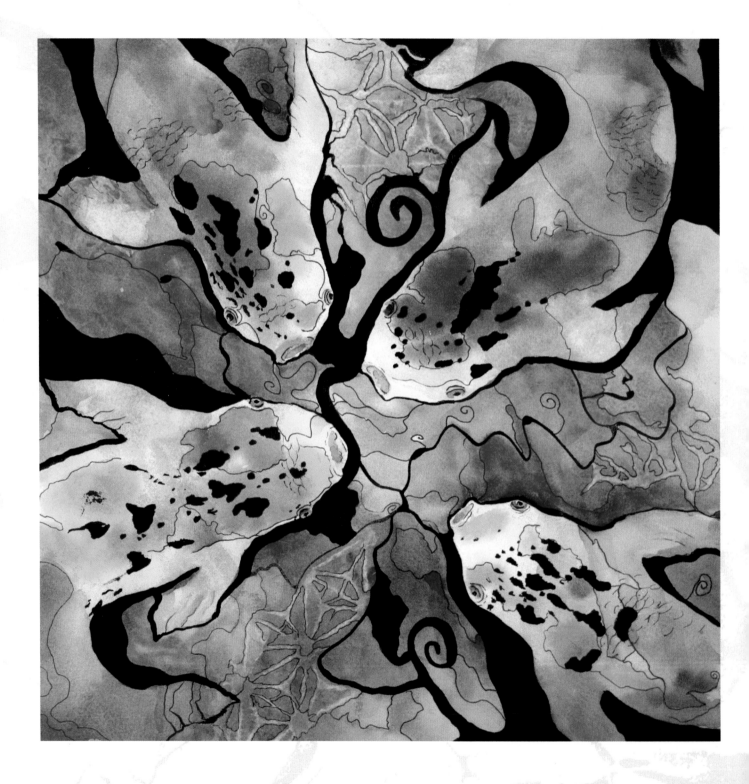

The fish in the lake detected the water stirring above them. The forest had begun to change. The trees continued to move as if alive, as if they were breathing. Leaves sparkled and flowers bounced to the beat of unheard music.

Vivid color and light continued to flicker through the bewitched woodland.

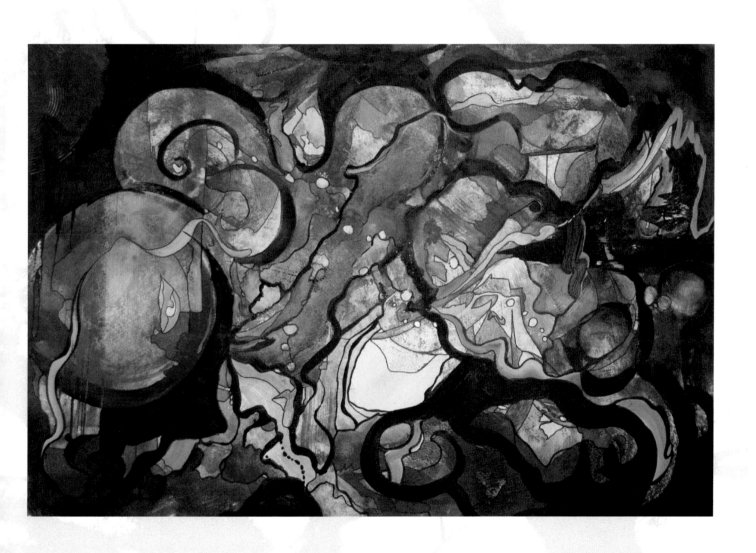

Above the pond waters the dragonfly spread her majestic wings and flew over the shimmering water leaving an iridescent trail behind her.

As the land shifted, more events began to occur.

Deep in the woods magical beings began to move about. In recent times these individuals were rarely seen, except by very perceptive people who could sense their presence. These creatures had been in the forest for thousands of years, but since the magnificent beauty of the woodland was forgotten and ignored, the mystical souls had become invisible over time and had been frozen in place.

They were amazed to be able to move with unanticipated freedom.

Some, like the Goose Goddess, were overwhelmed and shed tears of joy to be finally set free. All the ancient beings would now be visible to those entering the newly enchanted land.

To commemorate this eventful day, the tree people presented the fairy centaurs with a gift. They had fought many wars as enemies in the ancient forest.

"Let us live in peace and be grateful for this opportunity to once again live openly here in the wildwood," said the Tree King as he presented the Queen of the Fairy Centaurs an ancient crystal talisman.

"Yes, let us work together to make the forest what it once was," the Fairy Centaur Queen said as she accepted the glittering treasure.

The startled geese began to return and gathered near the compassionate Goose Goddess, whom they had not seen for many years. She tearfully embraced them as her children.

The forest now rumbled with new life and beauty.

Aeliana, the kind and powerful sorceress responsible for all this upheaval, smiled and surveyed the results of the spell she had cast.

Pleased with her work she mused, "Perhaps the forest will now be revered for all it has to offer and those who have come to take it for granted will once again cherish its dazzling beauty and begin to treasure their fellow beings."

But, as she contemplated the scene, Aeliana saw her work was not yet complete.

"Ah yes, I do not believe I have made my point yet," she said as she brandished her wand once more.

Suddenly the moon swirled around the earth, spun from the sky and landed at the bottom of the forest with a tremendous thud!

The ground shook. The animals were terrified and wondered if the sky was falling.

They talked among themselves wondering, "Is the world ending? What a terrible thing it would be if no one saw this beautiful forest because the end has come."

They waited a while, and nothing else seemed to be happening. Cinnamon Bear knew that the end had not come. He realized it was instead a new beginning for the forest.

"Do not be afraid little ones, all is well," he said with a curious smile.

Black Bear was very intrigued and bravely picked up the moon, gazing at the shiny orb. At that moment everything in the forest seemed to vibrate with amazing intensity.

As each of the animals emerged from their hiding places, they recognized the exquisite beauty of the world around them.

"How could we not notice this before?" said the Fox.

"We have never seen anything like this," said the Owl finishing with a nervous "Hoot."

The kind sorceress looked at them with great tenderness. She explained, "This beauty has always been here. You have not seen it, because you have forgotten how to look. But there is still something else you have not realized. Watch closely," she said.

"Oh no!" said the rabbit, fearfully heading back to the tree hollow.

At this moment the air cleared and the forest
shimmered with radiance.

The rabbit turned and stared in awe.

The cranes danced on the water in exaltation.

Everyone could see the change. From the tops of the trees to the bottom of the nearby ocean where sea turtles frolicked, enchantment reigned. The animals were impressed, and looked upon each other with great pride, "We are of this enchanted land, and we are all a part of this amazing forest. We are all joined to one another, and we are all beautiful."

They realized that they needed to have more compassion for each other. Suddenly aware of all of the magnificence around them, they began to understand that they all were joined as one, every being and plant was equally exquisite, each was as resplendent as the others, and each one was as vital as the others in composing this enchanted forest.

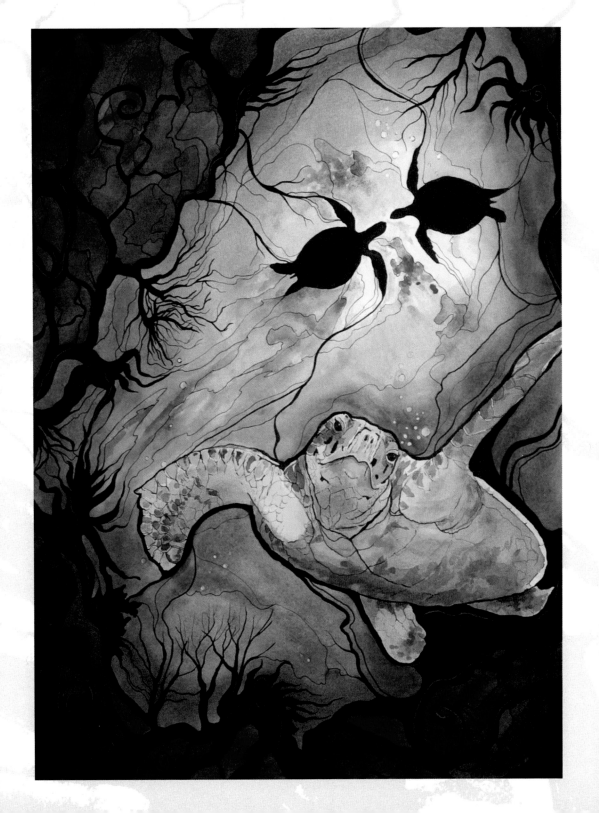

But, the Black Bear felt very sorry for the
shining moon that had been thrown
to the earth.
He said, "The moon is also a part of the
wonderment of the forest and it should not
sit on the forest floor where
only a few can see it."

And, because he now understood his own
power and the power held by every being on
earth, the Bear hurled the moon with all of
his strength up into the sky, where it landed
just above the Tree of Life. And there it
remained to light the night sky.

Aeliana was satisfied that all the creatures
had successfully received her message. And
after a moment of admiring the moon that
had been returned to the sky,
she had a revelation.

She thought, "If the full moon could
gradually disappear and then reappear
in the sky each month, its shining presence
would be a reminder of the lesson I have
imparted to all residing there."
She waved her wand once more, incanting
with the words...

Brilliant moon, bring your glorious light to shine
Making the darkness bright.

So they will remember, make your design
To go slowly when revealing your light.

Be sure they will recall the day
When the land was turned upside down.

Gradually change from a sliver of ray
To a full moon that lights like a crown.

To be certain that all take heed,
The darkness of the night abide,

Verify we have planted the seed, and
Be sure at least one night you hide.

Luna Transforma!

Looking at the new moon, with gentle knowing
expression, Aeliana said,
"My work is finished."

It came to pass that the most significant thing that happened in the enchantment of the forest was the effect that the woodland had on the people coming from the nearby towns and cities. After spending time in the newly created wildwood, absorbing its alluring elegance, they were reminded of their own connection to the land around them.

They realized that even their own towns and cities could be lovely places if they made the effort to take care of them.

Ultimately, they perceived the idea that they, as human beings, were an essential part of all nature. They soon learned to be stewards of all that surrounded them, always attempting to recreate the beauty that they had experienced in the Enchanted Forest.

Each time they returned from the mystical woodland they would share their new-found knowledge with those living in the urban areas, encouraging others to visit the Enchanted Forest and see for themselves.

The End

Paintings By Pattie Brooks Anderson
Illustrations in order of appearance:

1. Rumi's Trees © 2006
2. In Flight © 2008
3. Lady Bug, Lady Bug...© 2010
4. Lost In the City © 2009
5. The Alignment © 2011
6. Koi © 2009
7. Life Source © 2009
8. Magic Dragonfly © 2009
9. Goose Goddess Series I- Tears of Compassion © 2008
10. The Gift © 2008
11. Goose Goddess Series II - Mysterious Light © 2008
12. Soul Story © 2011
13. Spirit Bear, The Sky Is Falling © 2011
14. Holding the Moon © 2009
15. Owl's Prophesy © 2011
16. Crane's Walking © 2009
17. Sea Turtle's Plea © 2010
18. Tree of Life © 2010
19. Trillium Moon © 2010
20. Those Who Look But Do Not See... © 2009
21. Enchanted © 2008

Pattie Brooks Anderson

I believe drawing is one of the most profound methods to reach your own submerged artist. The way each person puts marks down on paper is different from any other individual. This acceptance of your personal mark-making is the validation of your own creative spirit.

When I get ideas for paintings, they sometimes come to me as complete images, usually during meditation or when I am walking in the trees or on the beach. Or they might be inspired by the colorful language in the practice of Qigong, one of my favorite pastimes. Other times, the image may materialize as I am painting with no subject in mind.

I feel that the painting is imparting knowledge to me. I often don't know why I am painting the image until I get close to completion and then the message becomes clear. It is often deeper and more complex than the simple image that is evident at first. I believe that these images and the subsequent messages are transmitted through a source greater than myself, or perhaps, from a part of myself that is connected to this source.

This is the alchemy that I believe happens with almost every painting that I do. I am left with a sense of wonder about the mysteries of our earthly experience and the sense of connection to something beyond our human existence. I love using animals, nature and whimsy to make this connection. Animals seem to impart a sense of spirit, and I never cease to be amazed at their ability to connect with us as human beings.

Made in the USA
Monee, IL
15 May 2022